A Merry Xmas 1926
& Elton.

# ROBIN HOOD

Then he drew the bow and loosed the shaft

# ROBIN HOOD

EDITED BY
GEORGE COCKBURN HARVEY, B.A.

ILLUSTRATED BY
EDWIN JOHN PRITTIE

THE JOHN C. WINSTON COMPANY, PUBLISHERS
PHILADELPHIA CHICAGO
TORONTO—THE JOHN C. WINSTON COMPANY, LIMITED

PRINTED IN THE U. S. A.

# CONTENTS

# CONTENTS

# LIST OF ILLUSTRATIONS

## INTRODUCTION

YET again may we withdraw from our work-a-day world into the cool, green delights of merry Sherwood forest, hearken to the three clear blasts of the bugle, and gladden our eyes as the five-score gay yeomen in Lincoln green troop to their master's call. Again may we hear the twang of the bow of yew and watch the gray goose shaft as it cleaves the glistening willow wand or brings down the king's proud buck. Again may we fare forth with the merry outlaw as in clever disguise he wins the archery prize of the haughty Sheriff of Nottingham and inveigles this personification of an oppressive tyranny into the ambuscade of the outlaw friends of the poor.

The spirit of eternal youth here frolics in an endless summer. Care-free and joyous, it relieves the haughty Norman of his gold and distributes its bounty to the poor and the afflicted. Its larders are always filled with good venison and brown October ale, and the feasts beneath the splendid oaks are one continuous picnic, enlivened by merry jests, rollicking songs, feats of strength, and contests with the good long bow. Over it all presides the gay Robin Hood, prince of outlaws and prince of men, who holds his sovereignty by the power of a character which exemplifies ideals that have sent the English race to enlighten the dark places of the earth and to proclaim a larger justice and a freer life to the victims of despotic oppression.

The charm of this inspiring personality has been a bond of sympathy between lovers of romance for a half dozen centuries. The greatest of all dramatists doubtless found here the inspiration for the forest of Arden with its dappled deer, its "life exempt from public haunt," its Amiens, the lineal descendant of Alan-a-Dale, its Jaques, an intellectual Friar Tuck, and its Orlando dividing with the Senior Duke the love and the rule of Robin Hood. Such a parallel may be too fanciful, but surely we shall rejoice that the most fertile romancer of the last century has in his greatest work summoned the aid of the valiant outlaws in his rescue of beauty in distress. Others will find rich ore in this same mine, and will coin its romance into rich treasures of the imagination.

Well may we rejoice in the glorious spirit of true sportsmanship personified by the merry outlaw. His was the nobility that fought a fair fight, refusing to use his waiting host against an honest foe; his the chivalry that never harmed a woman; his the generosity that could take defeat without malice and win to his band the victor by his large-hearted humanity. His sportsmanship lives in the best ideals of our games, in boy- and girl-scouting, in the splendid morale of our army and navy. Indeed, it may not be too much to say that the best spiritual demonstration of the last great conflict, so hardly survived, was this spirit that faces the vicissitudes of life and death neither to beg their favor nor fear their hate.

In this edition of Robin Hood an effort has been made to preserve the spirit of the old ballads. Occasionally a fantastic exaggeration has been toned down or omitted, but great care has been taken to give a true reflection of the distinctive and characteristic incidents of the old chronicle. The book is presented with an invitation to the reader to withdraw from the exacting round of our complex life and lose himself in the fine romance of merry Sherwood and its benevolent outlaws.

CHAPTER I

## HOW ROBIN HOOD BECAME AN OUTLAW

LONG, long ago, in the days when Henry the Second, first of Plantagenet Kings, was seated on the throne of England, a youth was walking swiftly through the forest of Sherwood. He was a tall, strong, comely lad, wearing a woodland dress of green jerkin and hose and a blue cap or hood on his head. At his shoulder swung a longbow of great strength, at his side was his sheaf of cloth-yard arrows,* and hanging at his girdle was a short woodknife.

The forest glade through which he strode was lined by huge oaks, and once he stood still to watch a herd of antlered deer sweep by in swift and graceful flight. One hand went to his bow, the other to his quiver, but he restrained himself, and forbore to lay an arrow on the string. For he knew that he was in a Royal forest, and that these were the King's deer, and to slay one was as much—nay, more—than a man's life was worth. More than a man's life, that seems a hard saying; but it is a true one.

*Arrows a yard long.

In those days one who killed a deer in a Royal preserve had his eyes torn out, and was mutilated in so dreadful a fashion that death would have been preferable.

The tall lad knew this very well; but another reason also caused him to stay his hand. He was on his way to Nottingham, hoping to enter the King's service as a Forester, and it would ill become one with his hopes to lay a hand on the Royal deer. He strode on, left the glade, and was crossing a piece of greensward, dotted by thickets of holly and coppices of hazelwood, when he was hailed by a harsh voice.

"Stand!" it cried. "Who art thou to march boldly through the King's greenwood?"

The lad turned, and saw a group of five or six figures beneath the shadow of a wide-spreading holly bush. All were seated on the ground save one, and he was the speaker. At a glance the youth knew them for a band of the King's Foresters, men who guarded the Royal preserve and the deer, and he saluted them with a motion of respect. Then he replied to the man who had accosted him, a man whose silver bugle horn showed that he was the Chief Forester.

"My name," said the tall lad, "is Robert Fitzooth, though many people call me Robin Hood. My parents are dead, and I am going to Nottingham."

"And why goest thou there?"

"I hope to become one of the King's Foresters."

The man laughed scornfully. "Easier said than done!" he growled. "Every landless man and masterless rogue longs to join our goodly company. Of what use to us would be such a stripling as thou art? We want a man, but thou hast naught save a man's bow."

" 'Tis more than a man's bow," cried another Forester. "Look at the strength of it. I trow that slip of a lad can never draw it."

"Draw it?" jeered the Chief Forester; "not likely. He does but carry it for vain pretense."

Robin's bright eye flashed, and his fresh face colored.

"I will draw it at a mark with any man among you," he cried.

"And what will you wager?" said the Chief Forester.

"I have no money," cried the fiery lad, "but I will lay my head against your purse that I hit any target you choose."

"Done!" cried the Forester angrily, "there's your target."

He pointed across the greensward to the mouth of a distant glade. A herd of deer had swept into view, and paused at sight of the men. They were led by a splendid hart, who now flung up his antlered head, snuffing the air and striking the ground impatiently with one forefoot. Robin Hood said nothing, but took his bow, tightened his string, and chose an arrow from his quiver. Then he laid his body into the bow in such fashion that the Foresters knew that here was no common archer, either in point of strength or skill. The great bow bent and tautened amid murmurs of wonder from the onlookers. Then Robin showed that he had nerve as well as great strength and skill. Just as he was drawing the steel head to the bow-shaft the Chief Forester cried out suddenly:

"'Tis your head you wager. Bethink thyself of that, my young friend!"

This was done to shake and disturb Robin just as he hung on his aim, but it failed. To all appearance the lad had heard nothing. His keen eye was glancing along the shaft, his brow was slightly furrowed in calculating thought, his lips were set firm; then twang! sang the bow-string, and the arrow hummed through the air like a great bee. And at the next instant the great beast made a leap into the air, and dropped on his side, dead, the shaft through his heart.

For an instant the Foresters were dumb with amazement at the wonderful shot; then murmurs of wonder arose. Robin turned quietly to the Chief Forester.

"I have won the purse," he said.

But the man smiled an evil smile. "I will tell thee what thou hast won," he said jeeringly; "thou hast won the pains and penalties of the forest laws. Yon was a King's hart royal, and so good a bowman as thou art must well know what it means for a man to slay a deer in the Royal forest. Seize him and bind him, my men."

Robin saw the fearful danger into which this hasty acceptance of the target had led him, and turned to fly. Too late! A couple of Foresters had already sprung on him. He was tripped up and borne to the earth, and in a trice his feet and hands were lashed together with bowstrings.

"Now we have a deer-killing rascal taken redhanded," chuckled the Chief Forester. "Twice or thrice of late the Sheriff hath complained to me that deer be stolen from the coverts, and yet we bring no rogue to be charged with the theft. This day we can content him."

Robin's blood ran cold as he heard these words. The treacherous villain had drawn him into the trap of shooting the deer, and now meant to give him up in cold blood as a common deerslayer, and to pretend that his capture was a proof of the keepers' vigilance.

The Forester's speech was hailed with shouts of applause from his underlings.

"Ay," cried one, "and let us take him in as such a knave should be carried!"

"How, Hubert?" demanded the Chief Forester.

"Why, bound in the hide of the deer he hath slain!" cried Hubert.

"Good!" cried his leader, "off with the hide, lads, and tie the rogue in it."

The knives of the Foresters made short work of stripping off the skin of the deer, and within a short time Robin was wrapped in the hot, greasy hide, the latter lashed across with spare bowstrings. The lad's head was thrust through an opening where the deer's neck had been, but of the rest of him there was but a shapeless bundle, enclosed in the soft dappled fur, which had so lately clothed the great stag. Robin's heart was bursting with rage and scorn for these mean traitors, but he was helpless. And the future was very black. The Norman Sheriff would never listen to a word that he might say; it was clear that an example was needed, and that he was to furnish it, and the picture rose before his eyes of the market place of Nottingham and himself under the hands of the hangman, who would carry out the dread sentence of the law. He had once seen a poor fellow suffer for this very offense that he was charged with, and he writhed again in agony to think that the punishment now hung over him. To hobble about for life, blind and a cripple, he who was now so young and strong, was too frightful a fate to dwell upon, and he twisted and turned in his bonds, and struggled to get free. But every effort was in vain. He was bound too securely for that.

"How shall we carry the knave in?" cried one of the rangers.

"Marry, but I have just thought of that, Dickon," replied the Chief Forester. "Did we not see two or three Saxon hinds* cutting wood a short half-mile from here as we came along? List, we can hear them now."

There was silence among the band, and the sound of axes rang from a distance.

"Run, Dickon," said the leader to the man who had spoken, "and bring them hither with the sled they had with them for dragging home the logs."

Away went Dickon, and in a short time he returned with the woodmen and their sled.

"Take up this knave," commanded the Chief Forester, "fling him on your sled, and drag him before us to the town."

The woodmen were three in number, and two hastened to obey, the third following more reluctantly. All three belonged to the poorest

*Laborers.

class of workers, and were dressed rudely in jerkins made of cowhide, with sandals and leggings of the same material, and no head covering on their matted shocks of hair. Two were old men, and these were swift to obey the command of the forest tyrants whom they feared; the third was a strongly built, square-shouldered fellow of some thirty years of age, who, as has been said, moved more slowly to obey the command. Among them, however, Robin was taken up and swung onto the sled, a framework of planks set on two wooden runners, the latter shaped from pieces of ash, which curved up naturally towards the fore part. Then the three hinds seized the ropes with which the sled was drawn along, and the rude carriage slid easily across the short, crisp grass.

Within half a mile they gained a rutted track, along which they turned, and now the sled bumped and jumped and tossed the deerhide bundle, with its human contents, from side to side. Robin was not flung completely off, because a row of posts stood up on either side of the sled, to prevent a burden being dislodged, but he was banged and bumped from side to side, utterly unable to help himself, while the brutal Foresters roared with laughter at the hopeless plight of their captive. The hide, too, was cramping Robin's limbs in dreadful fashion, and as it drew tighter moment by moment he could have cried out in agony. But he shut his teeth, and maintained silence, knowing that his groans would be music to the ears of his brutal captors.

Suddenly the course of the jolting sledge was interrupted. The Chief Forester sprang forward and brought his bowstave down with tremendous force across the shoulders of the young woodman.

"Ha, knave!" he cried, "thou dost not pull with a will. What, would'st thou show thy Saxon sullenness to us, the keepers of the forest!" And he rained a shower of blows on the man's head and shoulders.

The woodman's hand dropped to the handle of the short broad-bladed knife thrust in his girdle, but at a cry from one of the old men he withdrew it, and pulled as if he had been a horse which had felt the urging lash.

"Will, lad!" cried the old man, in trembling tone; "pull! pull! anger not the Forester."

"Ay, old man, you speak sooth," said the tyrant, with a savage laugh. "That advice is good, indeed. 'Twere well that Will should not anger the Forester. Pull, Will! Pull, dog of a Saxon!" and the Forester laid half a dozen hearty blows again on the young woodman. Beneath the fell of matted hair, the Saxon's eyes gleamed redly, but he bent his head to the storm, and pulled with a will in the most humble and obedient fashion. Presently a turn of the way brought them to a small hamlet of half a dozen huts, the largest of the houses being decorated with a bush hanging before the door.

"A tavern! A tavern!" cried Hubert. "What say you to a halt here, comrades! I trow I could empty a flagon after our long walk through the forest."

The others were of his opinion, and the sled came to a stand at the door of the little inn, while the Foresters called for wine.

As they stood there drinking, one of them suddenly raised a great shout.

"Look!" he cried, "yonder comes a band of our comrades, and see whom they have taken!"

Through the trees five more Foresters were approaching the hamlet, and among them marched two men, with hands bound and ropes fastened to their arms.

"Good, good!" cried the Chief Forester, in delight. "They have seized two of the outlaws who lurk in the forest. What with yonder rogues and the young scamp we have seized, the Sheriff will be heartily content. Bravely done, lads, how did ye seize them?"

Eager to hear how the outlaws had been taken, the Chief Forester and his men swarmed forward to meet the newcomers. They did not fear the escape of Robin Hood, lashed tightly in his wrapping of deer skin, and they did not dream that the Saxon woodmen would dare to make a movement without their permission.

Yet it was the old man who had called upon the younger woodman to be patient who was the first to flee. When he saw the Foresters turn aside, he dropped his rope, and fled softly away on his sandalled feet, like a dog that runs from the lash. He sprang into a narrow passage between two huts, and vanished. The second old man saw nothing of this. His back was turned to his comrade, and he stood stupidly gazing on the crowd of Foresters as they called to each other, laughing and talking, and some of the newcomers drinking from the flagons held out to them.

The young woodman, Will, made at first as if to follow his older companion, then cast a glance at the sled. Robin said nothing, lest he should call the attention of the Foresters, but his imploring eyes spoke for him. In reply Will dropped on one knee beside the sled, whipped out his broad, sharp knife, and slashed the bow-strings through with a few swift sweeps of the keen blade.

Robin was free. His bow and arrows had been laid beside him on the sledge to be brought in witness against him before the Sheriff, but now he caught them up, shot between two of the upright posts, and leapt after Will, who was dashing into the narrow passage between the huts.

"Hobb! Hobb!" called Will as he ran. "After us, man! After us!"

Hobb was the third woodman, the old fellow who stood gazing like an ox at the meeting of the Foresters. The warning cry drew his attention, and he looked round with a slow gape of wonder to see his comrades in flight. Unhappily, the voice of Will had caught ears for which it was not intended. The Chief Forester whirled on his heel, and gave a yell of anger at the sight which met his gaze.

"The knaves are fleeing!" he roared, in a voice of thunder, "and they have freed the captive. Back, lads, and seize them, alive or dead!"

He clapped an arrow on his bow as he spoke, and drew the string to his ear. Hobb was now lumbering after his friends, for at last his slow-moving wits had grasped the fact that a flight to the forest was the safest thing for him. But the grey-goose shaft was too swift by far. It hummed after him with the tremendous speed of an arrow just leaving the bow, struck him squarely between the shoulders, and he pitched forward on his face and lay still, the grey-goose shaft quivering as it stood upright from his back.

When Robin ran through the narrow passage between the houses he came to a small courtyard, over the further wall of which Will the woodman was already climbing: the old man had completely disappeared. Robin bounded across the little courtyard, put his foot on a crossbar of the wooden paling which formed the wall, and was over in a twinkling. Beyond lay a stretch of open ground, and across that the old man was running nimbly, with Will some distance behind.

Robin followed them at full speed, running his hardest for the shelter of the wood toward which his companions were making. He was just on the edge of the trees when he heard a shout behind him. He glanced back, and saw five or six heads spring to sight over the palisade. The Foresters were after them: but Robin shouted back a gay defiance, for among the woodland it would be difficult to track him, and he knew that he was within arm's length of safety.

He darted in among the trees, and saw Will a little before him, waiting for him to come up.

"This way! This way!" called the woodman, and Robin followed. At the next moment Robin saw the old man trotting along a narrow path, and the two younger men ran after their guide for some ten minutes. The old man led the way to a swamp, where he leapt from tussock to tussock of grass, warning the others to jump exactly where he did, or they would sink in the miry bog and be lost. Then they gained firm ground again, and the old woodman paused beneath a huge oak, and sat down to rest on a great root.

"Where's Hobb?" he panted.

"Dead, father," replied Will; "the Chief Forester took him with a shaft atween the shoulders. Hobb was slow to move."

"Ay, Hobb was always slow to move," returned the old man. "Well, well, his fate will be ours if e'er we come in reach of a Forester's long bow again. Ay, Will, I thought it was all up wi' ye when ye dropped your hand to your knife. Yon Chief Forester is indeed a hard and cruel man."

"It was naught but your words, father, that kept me quiet," replied Will. "It's hard to be beaten like a dog for nothing at all."

"Ay," said the old man, "we that once were holders of the land are treated as dogs, and worse than dogs, by our Norman masters. But we can never show our faces in the village again, Will. We must take to the forest, and hide there, or we shall soon be lodged in Nottingham jail, waiting for the rope and Master Hangman, as an example to all Saxon hinds who dare to disobey their masters."